This Book Belongs To:

Butler
Let your light
so shine!
♡ Sonya B.

ISBN: 978-1-7753583-8-1

 Published in Canada by WindyWood
Publishing of Nova Scotia.
Printed and bound by Marquis Printing,
Sherbrook Quebec

Dedication – author
Suzanne Sheehan

To Sarah and Jack: Thanks
for making storytelling so
much fun. Love you
always, you're the best!

Dedication – illustrator
Sonya Beeler

Thank you God, for my
family; my crown: Andrew,
Gaëlle, Jessica, Bruce and
Ted.

How the Blueberry Got its Crown

Suzanne Sheehan & Sonya Beeler

WindyWood Publishing . Hubbards N.S.

Once
upon
a time…

Sarah and Jack were picking
blueberries.

They worked hard to fill their buckets
and they ate a lot of berries! *Yum!*

Suddenly Jack made a face
and spit out a mouthful of berries.

"*Yuck! Those* taste awful!"

"Did you eat a bug?" asked Sarah.

"I don't think so," Jack told her.

He showed her a handful of berries.

"Where did you get those?" she asked.

"Over there," said Jack,
pointing to a patch of berries.

Sarah looked at them closely.

"I don't think those are blueberries," she said.

"They're blue berries, but not blueberries.
See, the leaves are different."

Sarah looked in her bucket.
"Oh, no! I think I picked some too."

Just then they heard a funny sound.

BOOOooooo
HOOooooo
Hooooooooo

"Did you hear that?" Sarah asked.

"It sounds like somebody crying."
Jack glanced around.

They looked down, and to their amazement, found a tiny fairy on a tree stump, crying her eyes out!

"Hey, who are you?" Sarah asked, kneeling by the stump.

Startled, the little fairy turned around.

"Oh! I'm Princess Merrystar Ferngully. Who are you?" she asked.

"I'm Sarah and this is my brother, Jack," Sarah told her. "Why are you crying?"

"Because…" wailed the little fairy, "Mummy told me not to wear my crown outside today. But it's so nice and sparkly…. I've lost it and she'll be upset with me. I was playing tag with a chipmunk and didn't realize my crown was gone!"

"We'll help you look for it," Sarah and Jack offered.

The tiny fairy brushed away her tears and brightened up. "Really? You'll help me find it? Oh, that's wonderful!"

Princess Merrystar jumped down.

Sarah and Jack and the Fairy Princess began to search the field of blueberries….

They looked **high** and saw clouds floating by and a seagull – but no crown.

They looked **low** and they saw lots of blooms and bugs and berries – but no crown.

They looked by the ocean but only saw a boat and waves....

No crown.

Finally, Sarah saw something sparkle in a beam of sunlight. There, caught on a blueberry bush, was the tiny crown!

"Found it!" Sarah shouted happily.

"Oh, thank you. Thank you! I'm so relieved…. I should have listened to Mum and not worn my crown out to play!"

"Well, I'm glad you found it," came a voice from behind them.

A beautiful fairy hovered at the children's eye level. She fluttered down to land beside the Fairy Princess.

"Oh, Mummy!" squeaked Princess Merrystar, "I didn't know you were there!"

The fairy gave her daughter a hug and a smile. "I know. I've been watching you to see if you needed my help, but you found it in the end. No harm done."

The beautiful fairy turned to Sarah and Jack, and introduced herself.

"I'm Rose, Queen of the Fairies. It was kind of you to help my daughter find her crown. I'd like to thank you. Is there anything I can do for you?"

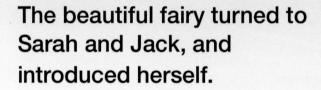

"Well," said Jack, looking in his bucket, "can you tell us which are blueberries and which aren't?"

The Fairy Queen examined the berries then plucked one from the bucket.

"This," she said, "is the berry from a wildflower. It doesn't taste very nice and it can make you sick. And this," she said, selecting another berry from the bucket, "is a blueberry."

"I don't see a difference," said Sarah, peering at the two berries.

"*Hmmmm*," said the Fairy Queen.
"I have an idea."

She set the berries down, pulled out her wand, and gave it a whirl.

Sparks flew from the end, forming a shimmering wave that rolled over the blueberry bushes. It disappeared beyond the crest of the hill and into the woods.

Magic swirled around them. The Fairy Queen turned to the children. "You helped my daughter find her crown, so I've crowned the blueberries for you."

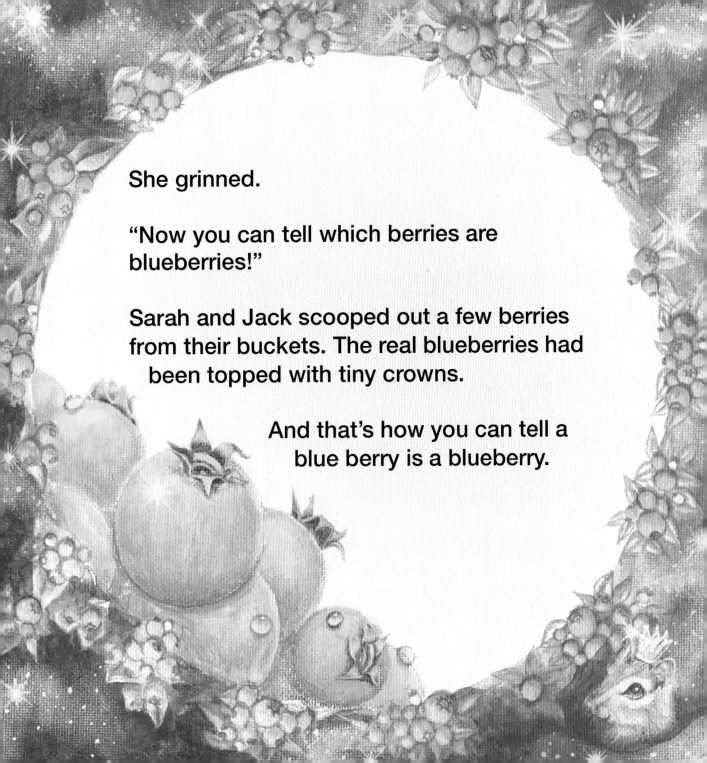

She grinned.

"Now you can tell which berries are blueberries!"

Sarah and Jack scooped out a few berries from their buckets. The real blueberries had been topped with tiny crowns.

And that's how you can tell a blue berry is a blueberry.

Delighted, Sarah and Jack thanked the Fairy Queen, said goodbye to their new friend, and headed for home.

ON THEIR WAY....

"Yum!" said Jack, munching on a handful of berries.

"Mum said she'd make Grammie's Blueberry Grunt when we get home – my favourite! What's your favourite, Sarah?"

Sarah thought for a moment.
"Wow, it's hard to decide! Probably Mum's blueberry muffins. But I love fresh blueberries best, especially now that they have fairy crowns!"

WHAT IS YOUR FAVOURITE WAY TO EAT BLUEBERRIES?

DELICIOUS
WILD BLUEBERRY RECIPES

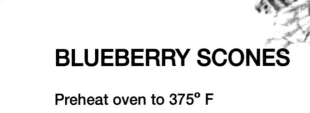

BLUEBERRY SCONES

Preheat oven to 375º F

2 cups flour
¼ cup sugar
1 tablespoon baking powder
½ teaspoon salt
½ cup cold butter
½ cup sour cream
3 tablespoons milk
1 teaspoon vanilla
grated zest from 1 orange
¼ cup fresh blueberries

Mix together the first 4 ingredients. Dice and cut in the butter until it resembles coarse crumbs. Combine the sour cream, milk, vanilla, and orange zest. Add to dry ingredients, mixing gently until just combined.

Divide dough into two equal portions. Pat into 9-inch circles. Sprinkle blueberries on one round, place the second round on top and press it firmly together. Divide into 12 wedges.

Bake at 375º F for 12 minutes or until top is golden brown.

– Suzanne

BLUEBERRY MUFFINS

Preheat oven to 400° F

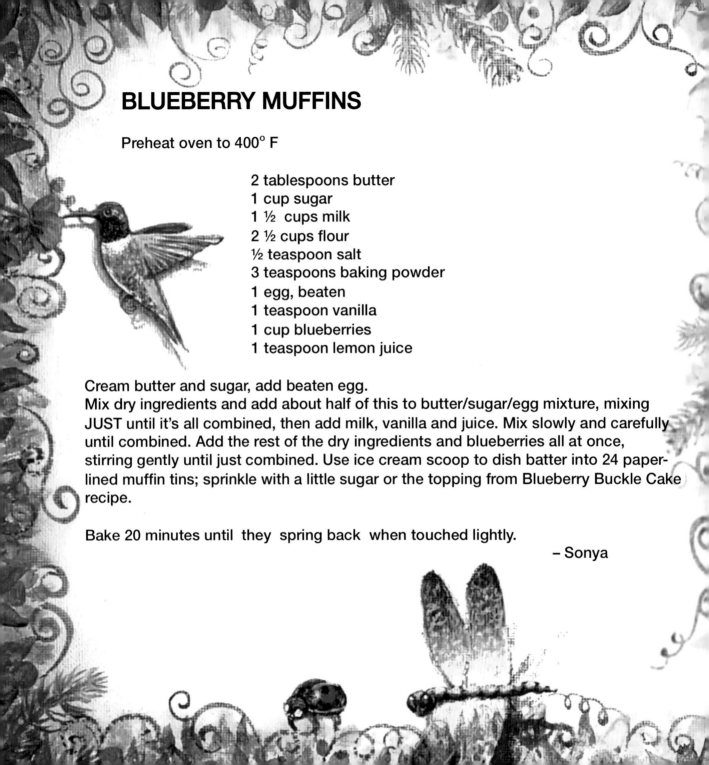

2 tablespoons butter
1 cup sugar
1 ½ cups milk
2 ½ cups flour
½ teaspoon salt
3 teaspoons baking powder
1 egg, beaten
1 teaspoon vanilla
1 cup blueberries
1 teaspoon lemon juice

Cream butter and sugar, add beaten egg.
Mix dry ingredients and add about half of this to butter/sugar/egg mixture, mixing JUST until it's all combined, then add milk, vanilla and juice. Mix slowly and carefully until combined. Add the rest of the dry ingredients and blueberries all at once, stirring gently until just combined. Use ice cream scoop to dish batter into 24 paper-lined muffin tins; sprinkle with a little sugar or the topping from Blueberry Buckle Cake recipe.

Bake 20 minutes until they spring back when touched lightly.

– Sonya

NOVA SCOTIA BLUEBERRY BUCKLE CAKE

Preheat oven to 350° F

½ cup butter or coconut oil
1 cup sugar
2 eggs, beaten
1 ½ cups flour
3 teaspoons baking powder
½ teaspoon salt
¾ cup milk or almond milk
1 teaspoon vanilla
2 cups blueberries

Topping:
⅓ cup sugar
½ cup flour
1 teaspoon cinnamon
¼ cup butter

Cream the butter and sugar together. Add the eggs. Add flour and baking powder and salt, then milk, vanilla. Scrape batter into a greased and floured or parchment paper-lined 8" square cake pan. Pour blueberries on top and THEN....

Mix the sugar, flour and cinnamon in a bowl. Add in the butter and squish with a fork until combined and crumbly. Sprinkle over batter. Bake 50-60 minutes or until a toothpick inserted into the centre comes out stained with blueberry but none of the white batter sticks.

– Sonya

BLUEBERRY GRUNT

Preheat oven to 400° F

    4 cups fresh or frozen blueberries
    ½ – ¾ cup sugar
    juice of ½ lemon
    *½ cup water if using fresh berries

Pour the blueberries into a deep-walled pan or cast iron skillet. Add water, sugar and lemon juice to the pot, stir thoroughly, cover, and bring to a boil over medium high. Then reduce heat to medium. Boil 15-20 minutes until there's plenty of juice. While this is cooking, make the dumplings.

Dumplings:

    2 cups flour
    4 teaspoons baking powder
    ½ teaspoon salt
    1 teaspoon sugar
    1 tablespoon butter
    1 tablespoon shortening
    ¼ – ½ cup milk

Sift the flour, baking powder, salt and sugar into a bowl. Cut in the butter and shortening, and add enough milk to make a soft biscuit dough. Drop spoonfulls of the mixture on top of the hot blueberry mixture. Cover with lid or aluminum foil, reduce heat to low, and do not peek for 15 minutes. You will likely hear grunting noises. Serve hot with ice cream or whipped cream.

Note: If you prefer the dumplings browned, preheat the oven to 400° F degrees. After steaming the grunt, place the open pan in the oven for 10 – 15 minutes to brown them.

– Catherine Sheehan

BLUEBERRY SAUCE

– for pancakes or ice cream

½ cup sugar
1 teaspoon butter
2 tablespoons cornstarch (+additional 1tablespoon if using for pie filling)
1 teaspoon lemon juice
1 cup blueberries

Combine ½ cup sugar with 2 tablespoons cornstarch in a 2- or 4-cup glass measuring cup or bowl. Add 1 teaspoons lemon juice and 1 cup blueberries. Mix together lightly. Microwave for 2 minutes, stir, then microwave 1 minute more. Stir and repeat until thickened and bubbly. Add 1 teaspoon butter.

Store in a jar in the fridge. If you add 1 extra tablespoon of cornstarch in the beginning, you can use this as a nice filling for tart shells.... Makes delicious little emergency blueberry pies.

– Sonya

Author
SUZANNE SHEEHAN

Suzanne Sheehan comes from a family of creative people, including artists, sewers, crafters, gardeners, and storytellers. She has fond memories of her grandmother and mother reading and telling stories to her and her sister, and continued the tradition with her own children. This book is the first story she ever told her children, Sarah and Jack.

Suzanne tends to see the bright side of life, has a wide range of interests, and a silly sense of humour. She lives in a small rural community on the shore of the Bay of Fundy, on a hobby farm with her family, two dogs, two cats, and a small flock of chickens. She works in Human Resources.

Illustrator
SONYA BEELER

Sonya Beeler has loved art since early childhood, surrounded by her father's books and brilliant, realistic paintings and drawings. She delighted in visiting her grandmother's turpentine-scented basement apartment and admired the delicate paintings of blueberry bushes, lady slippers, bulrushes and toadstools, under which, her grandmother assured her, dwelt faerie folk. During her career in banking, she enjoyed writing, illustrating and telling stories to her four children, to their classmates and now to her precious grandchildren. Sonya feels very honoured to have been able to illustrate this beautiful, imaginative story.

To see more of Sonya's work, visit sonyambeeler.blogspot.ca

Nova Scotia Wild Blueberries

Wild blueberries, Nova Scotia's number one fruit crop in acreage, production and export value have grown naturally in the Maritime Provinces, Quebec and the state of Maine for thousands of years.

When the blueberry bush's blossoms are pollinated by bees and other insects as they fly from flower to flower then the base of the flowers grow into blueberries.

Wild blueberries are harvested from early August to mid-September. The berries are rich in anthocyanins. Their superior taste and versatility have created demand for Nova Scotia's wild blueberries all over the world.

Photos and information on wild blueberries provided courtesy of the Wild Blueberry Producers Association of Nova Scotia.